BEYOND BELIEF

EDITED BY DONNA SAMWORTH

First published in Great Britain in 2023 by:

Young Writers
Remus House
Coltsfoot Drive
Peterborough
PE2 9BF
Telephone: 01733 890066
Website: www.youngwriters.co.uk

Book Design by Ashley Janson

Softback ISBN 978-1-80459-738-5

Printed and bound in the UK by BookPrintingUK
Website: www.bookprintinguk.com
YB0MA0024B

Foreword

Welcome, Reader!

For our latest competition A Twist in the Tale, we challenged primary school students to write a story in just 100 words that will surprise the reader. They could add a twist to an existing tale, show us a new perspective or simply write an original story.

The authors in this anthology have given us some creative new perspectives on tales we thought we knew, and written stories that are sure to surprise! The result is a thrilling and absorbing collection of stories written in a variety of styles, and it's a testament to the creativity of these young authors. Be prepared for shock endings, unusual characters and amazing creativity!

Here at Young Writers it's our aim to inspire the next generation and instill in them a love of creative writing, and what better way than to see their work in print? The imagination and skill within these pages are proof that we might just be achieving that aim! Congratulations to each of these fantastic authors.

Contents

The Stories

THE ALIEN INVASION

This is the story of the alien invasion.
The alien invasion started on the 18th of January 2222 because the world decided to skip 200 years. I don't know why. The aliens decided to get rid of the snow. They were allergic.
The aliens came on 17th January 2222 and they made some changes which were: No more food, just food pills, more water and washing your hands.

Grace Lee (10)
All Saints Benhilton CE Primary School, Sutton

JAZZY

Once upon a time, there was a girl called Jazzy. She always wore a black shirt and white jeans. Early one morning, her grandpa said, "Take this basket of food to your sister, but whatever you do, don't run."

So Jazzy hopped and she hopped until she was in the middle of the jungle. The jungle was dark and smelt horrible, so she couldn't see or smell the trees. Along came the fox.

"Where are you going?" he asked and Jazzy explained. Unfortunately, there was a tiger listening to everything. He went to find her sister's house...

Emma Kirvejova (8)

Bantock Primary School, Pennfields

LILLY TILLY'S WORST ENDING

Once upon a time, there was a little girl called Lilly Tilly. She had a friend called Emily.
One day, her mum said, "Go visit your uncle."
Her uncle's house was in the forest. She didn't mind, so she still went.
When she got there, Emily was there with a girl. They looked suspicious, so she spied on them and heard them talking about their evil plan. She'd had enough and confronted them. They were shocked. Then they started fighting. It never ever stopped. It went on and on and on until they all got tired.

Bettina Nyari (8)
Bantock Primary School, Pennfields

THE CANDY AND UNICORN LAND

Once upon a time, there was a cute little girl called Areena who loved fun adventures. She was also very fond of sweets.
In the afternoon, Areena got very tired, so she went to her room and got in bed to nap.
When Areena woke up, she found herself sleeping on cotton candy instead of her own bed. In fact, she was in a whole new world. It was filled with candy, sweets and unicorns. Areena went to explore. Suddenly, Areena tripped over a jelly bean and fell into a deep hole.
She woke up. It was just a dream.

Aleena Mohammed Fowzul (8)
Bantock Primary School, Pennfields

THE HUNGRY BOY

Once upon a time, there was a boy who ate goats. But one day, his father said there were no goats to eat. So the boy went across the river to the other side of his uncle's farm, but there were no more. He was upset, but then a miracle happened. There were two sheep about to get eaten by a bear. The boy ran as fast as he could to get the sheep. He didn't care if he had to fight a bear. They had a fight and he won.
He went back home and his family enjoyed it.

Anil Kumar (8)
Bantock Primary School, Pennfields

TRIXI THE TEDDY

One sunny morning, there was a cute little teddy bear in the quiet bedroom. The cute little teddy bear's name was Trixi. The cute teddy bear got off the shelf. She crept on the soft floor.
Suddenly, the girl woke up and saw Trixi.
Surprised, she said hello. The cute teddy bear asked if they could be friends.
The girl said, "Of course."
They played all day with the girl's toys. Suddenly, they heard a noise coming from downstairs. It was Mummy. So she hopped into bed with Trixi and pretended to sleep.

Layne Stanley (7)
Barlaston First School, Barlaston

THE GOAT'S SECRET

The three Billy Goats Gruff trudged across the sunny field.
"That troll must be hiding something, he always goes missing," Big Goat said with suspicion.
"We should go under the bridge," the other goats explained.
It took some time to convince Big Goat but he finally agreed. Tiptoeing to the bridge, they fell into a secret trap.
"Ahaha! You really tried to find my secret base," Troll shouted.
They begged for mercy, but the troll took off his mask.
"Hahaha! It's me, Billy Goat Gruff Junior."
"That's not funny," they all agreed.
And the mystery was solved safely!

Aaminah Akhtar (10)
Brockholes Wood ASC, Preston

THE FOUR LITTLE PONIES

The four little ponies were playing on a field.
Galloping through the grasslands, the little
Shetland ponies hopped in joy as the shire horses
came, but they should not have. One of them
tripped, then the other, then another. Waking up
from the huge bump, they teleported to the moon!
As the stars danced on top of them, they worried
as they couldn't breathe. They jumped off...
teleporting back to Earth. Shock filled their bodies
as their eyes lit up in horror as they saw a ghost.
As the Shetlands came back to Earth, the horses
were happy once again.

Jayde Davies (10)
Brockholes Wood ASC, Preston

RAPUNZEL AND THE EVIL PRINCE

Once, there was a girl called Rapunzel. When she was little, an evil woman took Rapunzel off her mother. Rapunzel and her evil, mischievous stepmother were living in a big tower. It was so high that Rapunzel could not get down. But luckily for her, she had long, luscious hair. And she normally climbed down her hair. One day, Rapunzel met a prince. He looked nice, but little did she know he was evil. The prince trapped Rapunzel in his house. She luckily escaped and found her real mother. Rapunzel lived with her mum. They lived happily ever after.

Brooke Black (9)
Brockholes Wood ASC, Preston

THE EVIL MAYOR

"Argh..."
In the middle of the clouds, a dragon king and dogs with bodyguards were protecting the king's money, but one of the guards was nice and sometimes he let children rob the king's money. One day, the children jumped into the ocean to go to a mysterious cave with a portal that led to the Atlantic City. The children gave the money to the mayor of the Atlantic Ocean. Suddenly, the three-headed dragon and the mayor had a fight! The three-headed dragon fell to the bottom of the ocean...

Ethan Downse (8)
Brockholes Wood ASC, Preston

A BIRTHDAY SURPRISE

Once, there was a girl called Stacey.
Her mum said, "Do you want to go swimming?"
She said, "Yes, I would love to go."
Then Stacey and her mum went to the beach and her mum went to the ocean and then a shark came by and had a fish for them to eat for dinner. Then, when they came back home, they saw that their kitten had died. Stacey was crying and her mum bought her a new one and Stacey's birthday was the next day.
"Surprise!"

Wiktoria Deyk (10)
Brockholes Wood ASC, Preston

HAUNTED HOUSE GONE WRONG

One day, there were two little kids walking in the forest. They walked past a mysterious house, but the kids liked the house and decided to go in it. All of a sudden, they heard a crash and decided to go upstairs. They saw what made the crash, it was a cat. They suddenly saw it, but only a glimpse of it. It was a killer and it screamed, but it was their friend and they got ice cream to eat for dinner. The kids still have it coming for them, not happily ever after...

Leyah Sumner (8)
Brockholes Wood ASC, Preston

THE GINGERBREAD MAN'S GREAT ESCAPE

One day in a village, an old person cooked a gingerbread man but she found out it was alive and it ran away. The old lady chased it everywhere, then a hungry, starving cow chased him with more drooling animals around the empty farm. When he was running, a fox came and he thought he was going to eat him, but instead saved him and he ran off from the people with the fox. They built a big Lego mansion and lived happily ever after with nobody disturbing them.

Rylan Smith (10)
Brockholes Wood ASC, Preston

GOLDILOCKS AND THE THREE BEARS

Most children would run for their lives when they saw the three bears but not Goldilocks! She stayed with the bears and helped them to build comfy beds and new comfy chairs, and she showed them how to make porridge that was just right. They all lived happily ever after!

Alina Ishtiaq (10)
Brockholes Wood ASC, Preston

THE UNKNOWN RULER

We will be announcing the prime minister on 25/12/22 so get ready. Nobody knows about me, only my name, Meerab. Everyone waits irresistibly.
"What do you think she looks like?"

"I dunno but she's definitely in her twenties."

"Maybe, but the rules and things she's doing are amazing, I can't wait to meet her!"
Everybody is going to see me now, what shall I do?
They will all be surprised it's an eleven-year-old girl.
Just then, the speakers go on, "Meerab is now here!"
"Hello!" I shout.

The crowd screams and everyone looks in shock and happiness.
"*A kid?*"

Meerab Saleem (11)
Coston Primary School, Greenford

PINOCCHIO'S LONG NOSE

Pinocchio lived in a village. Pinocchio was very kind but mostly greedy. Sometimes he did good and bad deeds.

One day, Pinocchio asked his father, "Why do I have a long nose and you have a short nose?"

"Well, it's a long story."

"Can you tell me the story?" asked Pinocchio.

"Are you sure?"

"Yes!"

When his father said just one word, Pinocchio vanished. When Pinocchio woke up, *he was Cinderboy at the stadium*. He had the ball so he had to get a goal. He ran and... *Boom!* He scored and vanished again. Pinocchio couldn't believe what had happened.

Adam Harasa (8)

Coston Primary School, Greenford

HANNAH AND GREG

Once upon a time, there lived Hannah, Greg and their parents. Since their stepmother hated them, she made a very evil plan with her husband. The next day, she called the children to come outside and said they were going berry picking.
"You must not come back until midnight!" she ordered.
It was late and they needed a place to stay. They met a kind witch. But Hannah was hungry. Suddenly, Hannah started to chase the witch. They ran around the table, knocked over chairs and broke some plates. Yet Hannah and Greg were still able to eat her ravenously!

Maweyda Abdullahi (9)
Coston Primary School, Greenford

LITTLE LADYBUG

Once, there lived a small ladybug called Winy. She had ninety-nine spots and always sat on a red leaf. Winy was dreaming about green leaves. One day, she decided to go to the green forest full of beautiful trees, bushes and colourful leaves. As Winy was strolling along, she met the ugliest insect. Winy and the insect started to play together. Suddenly they were trapped in a spiderweb. They couldn't get out and were shaking because it was night and cold. Luckily, in a second, a secret sparrow ripped off the web and rescued the insects. They became good friends!

Nel Pieniążkiewicz (6)
Coston Primary School, Greenford

THE FIELD TRIP

Zack got on the bus with Mary, they were going on a field trip to the funfair. When they got there, it didn't look like a funfair, they were at an abandoned house. They walked inside. They heard a strange noise.

"Come here," said a shadow.

They walked closer and closer until... *Boom!* A gunshot. As they walked towards it, they saw that it wasn't a gunshot, it was something falling. Then they chased after the shadow, but as they got close, it disappeared. They went back to school and thought it was nothing. Then they saw it!

Angel Mae McDonald (9)
Coston Primary School, Greenford

THE SECRET SPY

One day, a football organisation called FIFA announced a tournament called Brazil World Cup. Most countries would play football to be the winner. The tournament was only for men, but little did they know there was a woman called Lilly Stone. She disguised herself as a man and played football with the other teammates. Nobody knew she was a woman but at the same time, she was a spy. One football match, she took out a magic gadget and sent a player into a portal! Would the representatives discover that she was an evil spy working for Agent 46?

Natan Pieniążkiewicz
Coston Primary School, Greenford

THE MYSTERIOUS PERSON

There was a sweet little girl called Lilly. She was sleeping peacefully at night when suddenly there was a scratch on the door. Her parents weren't at home so she woke up and went downstairs and opened the door. *Woosh!* A cat came running in. She screamed in terror and then she looked at the cat and went down to touch it. It was a black and white cat with blue eyes. She went to hold it. Suddenly, a cloud of black dust appeared around the cat. Then the cat turned into a human figure, then vanished into thin air...

Pukalana Johnrohan (10)
Coston Primary School, Greenford

THE TEDDY BEAR THAT CAME TO LIFE

Once upon a time, there was a princess that had a teddy bear that she loved. She would always play with it and never leave it alone. But one day she left it on her table. When she went back, she saw it on the floor so she quickly picked it up and went downstairs to get a snack. Then she sneakily looked at her doll and saw it moving, so she quickly ran downstairs and took it to her friends' house. Her friends got scared and ran away. She locked the doll up and pretended it never happened.

Areesha Saleem (6)
Coston Primary School, Greenford

THE BEAR WHO ATE A GIRL

In a deep, dark, wild forest was a little girl named Rily. She found herself in the forest. She woke up and gasped, there was a huge bear staring at her. She ran home but it was too late, the bear kept catching her. Rily stopped and saw her house broken. Rily didn't know what to do, the bear kept catching her, so she went to the back of the house. He didn't see her. She ran after the bear while thinking about where to go. Just then, she woke up from her dream...

Aizah Saleem (8)
Coston Primary School, Greenford

A MONSTER IN THE WOODS

One day at a school called Nevermore High, a student named Tyler went into the woods like he usually did and didn't come back. The students thought it was fine and that he'd just gotten lost, so they didn't bother about it.
A student was going to the nearby town but they heard something in the woods. There was a scream and something huge came out of the woods. It went into the school and started to kill everyone.
Suddenly, a student transformed into a werewolf and almost defeated the monster. Then the monster ran away.

Gavin Stevenson (11)
Crawforddyke Primary School, Carluke

MYSTERY HORSE STORY

In 2005, there was a horse called Frank and his owner was called Bella. She was a showjumper, and at the time, she was the best.
One day, they were flying to Brazil for a show, and when they got there, Bella went to her hotel because it was late and her trainer took Frank to his stable. Everything was fine until the morning. Bella got a call from her trainer. Her horse was gone. He was not in his stable...

Ellie Mcdowall (11)
Crawforddyke Primary School, Carluke

UNUSUAL WORLD

"Stop complaining, class, I've had enough of your nonsense! History is not boring, it's fascinating." All of the students automatically paid attention, except Usibella who fidgeted while imagining the teacher's horrible fate. "King William the Ninth was crowned in Bucket Palace in London on..."
As blah blah blah droned on, Usibella doodled her vision of London in the past: smartphones, red buses, Canary Wharf.
Looking outside for inspiration, she gazed at the rippled, purple moon shooting across the sky. It was morning at last!

Nailah Islam (10)
Cubitt Town Primary School, Isle Of Dogs

ON THE RUN!

My heart is in my mouth. "Stop that boy!" they scream. I bump into people. I run down an alleyway. Dead end! I pull onto a pipe and climb over the shed. They're still onto me! Beads of sweat form on my forehead. I try to outrun them. Their arms are outstretched, but there is nothing I can do.

"Stop that thief now!"

I jump behind a barrel, breathing hard. "Where did that boy go?" I hear them yelling. A hand reaches down and grabs me. "This isn't a master thief! It's a girl!"

"Yep, that's me!"

Lily Kirsch (10)

East Claydon School, East Claydon

THE POSITIVE GYMNAST

Amelie was sad. At her last gymnastics competition, she broke her wrist. It had hurt lots. She had trained hard and couldn't show what she could do. She was devastated. At hospital, the doctor said Amelie had to have a cast on her arm and couldn't do gymnastics for two months.
Amelie was determined to recover, work hard and make her next competition.
On the day of the competition, she got butterflies in her tummy, but she stayed positive. Amelie won her event on the bars!
Even when you have a setback, just stay positive and you can succeed.

Sienna Leafe-Williams (9)
East Claydon School, East Claydon

THE BEWILDERING BOOK

I had just arrived in Florida and I heard shouting coming from everywhere.
"Flood! Flood!" It was noisy. When I stepped into the deep cavernous water, I looked carefully. There was a library with no water filled in it. It was really shocking but when I entered, I had nothing to explain. It was as warm as the sun. I felt so snug and congenial that I nearly fell asleep. Anyway, I was finding some books when I felt a pinch on my finger and I suddenly arrived at a mysterious sibylline book...

Manreet Jheetey (10)
East Tilbury Primary School, East Tilbury

LILLY AND LAYLA PLAY HIDE-AND-SEEK

Lilly: "Layla, do you want to play hide-and-seek with me?"
Layla: "Yes, I do."
They both play. Lilly counts, Layla hides.
Lilly: "One, two, three, ready or not, here I come."
One hour later, Lilly said, "Come out please, I don't want to play anymore."
One week later, "Come out, please. I've had enough."
"Where's Layla?" said Mr Williams, Lilly and Layla's father.
"I don't know," said Lilly.
"We have to try and find her!" said Mr Williams.
One day later, "Finally, we found you!"
"How many days were you there for?"
"8 days."
"Oh my god," said Mr Williams.

Aziza Javed Noorafsa Ashrafi (8)
Eastbury Community School, Barking

GOLDILOCKS AND THE THREE BEARS

Once upon a time, Goldilocks and her mum were baking cakes and candies.
Later, they got tired and slept in their beds.
Five minutes later, the three bears entered the house and saw the cakes and candies.
In the blink of an eye, Goldilocks and her mum were downstairs. They were surprised and they had a party.

Maryam Butt (7)
Eastbury Community School, Barking

THE CANDY COTTAGE

Sleeping Beauty and her prince lived in a cottage in the woods and lived very happily, until they had twins, as sadly Sleeping Beauty died. Her husband kindly looked after them and named the kids Hansel and Gretel.

One day, they went out to the forest and got lost. Hansel and Gretel wandered around, then Hansel cried out, "I see smoke!" Both walked round a tree and saw a cottage, not their cottage but one made out of candy!

Outside, they saw an old lady. She spotted them and exclaimed, "My, you must be lost! Come and eat!"

Leilani Ti-i Taming (8)

Emmanuel Community School, Walthamstow

ESCAPE TO NORWAY

One day in Ukraine there were children called Ben and Mary. They were sent out of Ukraine, even though they didn't want to. They went to Norway in a small city in a big house. Soon as Ben opened it to their surprise it was big and filled with maids. As soon as they got to the staircase a man with a bushy beard said hello.

Mary said, "What's your name?"

"I am Peter, one of your mom's friends. Okay? Come with me to your bedrooms."

Ben got a king bedroom because he was the oldest.

Sean Chikunga (8)

Emmanuel Community School, Walthamstow

THE BIRTH TO DEATH OF A DANCER

Hmm, what about breakfast? Hmm, I want eggs.
Help! Oh no, Mother! Oh no, whaa!
Twelve years later, Princess Cece and Lilyana, her little sister, went to their birthday party. They were so excited because CeCe, Nina and Lilyana were going to have an audition to see who would be the black swan for ballet.
CeCe was picked. She had to do a dance. While she was dancing a boy with knives came flying and CeCe dodged him and finished her dance.
Lily gave her tea. CeCe drank it and she passed away.

Abigail Amoanimah Frimpong (8)
Emmanuel Community School, Walthamstow

THE TITANIC WITH A TWIST

A ship was sent to America. A man, a lady and two kids followed her. In the distance, there was a big block of ice. They all screamed, "Iceberg!" once or twice.
They crashed into the iceberg then out came a caveman. All they had to shoo it away with was a tin can. Before they could throw it the ship sank. The passengers found it hard to survive.
Then along came a shark. They all started to hide. A whale came. All the people floated into its mouth. The whale took them to the south.

Sienna Dalson (8)
Emmanuel Community School, Walthamstow

SNOW WHITE

There was a lady and she did not want to get a child. But then she said out the window, "Please do not give me a girl with as white as snow and hair as black as coal and lips as red as blood."
Exactly that happened. Then she said to her soldier to take her away in five years.
Five years later, the soldier tried to take her but then she yelled, "I am not going!" She ran away and hid.
After, her mum died and she got a nice new mother. She lived happily ever after.

Janneke Kramers (8)
Emmanuel Community School, Walthamstow

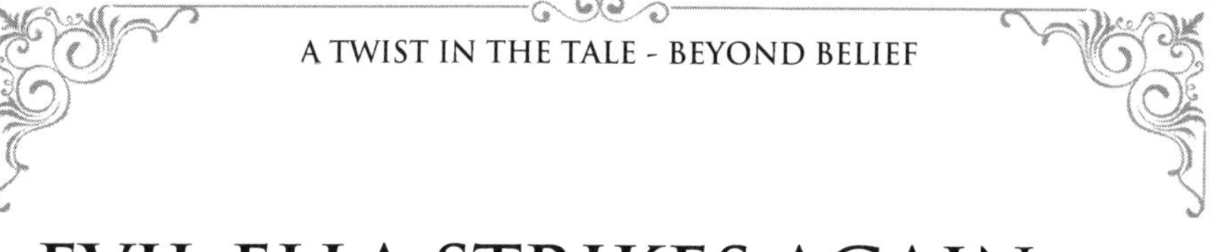

EVIL ELLA STRIKES AGAIN

"Give it to me!" said Evil Ella. She took the marbled ball to her lair and she looked for its magic. She could finally visit the Nevermore forest! The Nevermore forest was only for the strongest of villains! "Yes, I've finally got to Nevermore Forest!" Ella took off her mask and revealed her true identity! Evil Ella had become Enchanted Ella. She needed to get her village back, but not how it is now, old Nevermore - the fairy land, the mermaid lake, the great elf tree. Now she had the chance to do so. Nevermore Forest was back.

Maicie Dinham (11)
Falconbrook Primary School, Battersea

THE TEDDY BEAR

Once upon a time, a boy named Mical lived in a small apartment and he was in debt since his parents left him. Luckily, his parents left him some decorations to decorate his house.
One day he went to his basement and something caught his eye. Teddy. It gave him a feeling of nostalgia. He picked it up and roots started growing on the walls then a teddy bear monster emerged and chased him. He left the basement and ran across the hallway. It was infinite. He saw a weapon and grabbed it.
He tripped and woke up horrified.

Isaac Mosengo (10)
Falconbrook Primary School, Battersea

FLEUR'S UNEXPECTED WALK

Fleur the golden retriever was lost in the woods. Suddenly, she heard loud footsteps, footsteps coming towards her. *Oh no*, thought Fleur, and she ran as fast as she could. Birds flew out of her way when she darted past like a horse trying to win a race. Only Fleur was not racing, she was escaping from extreme danger. Rain splattered against her soft, beautiful coat and mud sprayed behind her but she kept on going, however, the rain got heavier. She started running out of energy.
Fleur turned around... and there with tears in their eyes was her owner.

Rachel Roper (10)
Frogmore Junior School, Frogmore

A DISGRACE TO PUBLIC

SuperSanaa, famously known as SS, stepped into the grassland. The war commenced in 3... 2... 1...
Phweee!
After thrashing each other around, V (the villain) surrendered! In V's sanctuary, SS and V met up and created a master plan! From that day onwards they sent secret messages.
One particular day, the MI (Mythical Islands) vanished into thin air. Historians believe SS betrayed the public and was always a villain...

Teshvi Gottipati (10)
Frogmore Junior School, Frogmore

LITTLE WEE BEAR AND GOLDIE

Waking up from my slumber, I ran downstairs for my daily porridge, but it was too hot. So I went for a stroll in the woods.
Then I returned home and it was upside down.
"I'm sure Dad locked the door. Let's go and see. Probably a thief or something. Look, my porridge has been eaten and we left the spoons in the middle. My chair's broken! Ugh! There are footprints going upstairs. Who is this in my bed? Let's scare her." *Rahhhh!*
She jumped out of the window. She was never seen again. That girl was really impudent!

Laura Bonio (9)
Gardners Lane Primary School, Cheltenham

THE RAIN IN MANCHESTER

"Why are you putting my friends in the oven?" stuttered Jack.
"I don't have any friends," sobbed the giant.
"I can be your friend," whispered Jack. "You have to let them go first!" demanded Jack.
The giant pulled Jack's friends out one by one.
"Jack, come down for your tea and bring your friends, it's getting cold!" shouted Jack's mum.
"Promise you will come back. I am so lonely," cried the giant.
"I promise," smiled Jack with his fingers crossed behind his back. He never returned again.
The giant sobbed and sobbed. It never stops raining in Manchester now.

Aaron Seddon (11)
Garrett Hall Primary School, Tyldesley

THE LAIR

Something was off about this place. Something more sinister than I thought...
"I don't like it here," Talia muttered under her breath.
"Me neither!" I replied with butterflies in my stomach.
"Let's get out!" Talia replied rapidly.
Climbing out the dark, damp hut, I realised the monster wasn't in their lair... so where was the monster?
Roar! There was a grumble that made me sick to my stomach. When I heard it I ran. But where did Talia go...?
Suddenly, a gushing pain ran through my back. Blood gurgled out, covering my face. *Goodbye, cruel world...* I thought to myself.

Alessia Lloyd (10)
Garrett Hall Primary School, Tyldesley

WHAT'S THAT ROCK?

Once there were two dragons on a planet far away. One was kind to everyone and shy (named Anya) and her best friend (Olive) was brave and extremely crazy.
One day, the two dragons went into the woods to play some games but Olive noticed something.
"What's that?" she asked, confused.
"I don't know. I think it's sparks," stuttered Anya.
They followed the sparks and found a rock that made everyone kind. Olive knew this because she'd read it in a book. As they raised the mysterious rock up, kindness conquered the azure planet.

Jessica Atherton (10)
Garrett Hall Primary School, Tyldesley

DANGER IN THE GRAVEYARD

One cold December night, I was walking my dog and I decided to walk a different way than usual. Little did I know this wasn't a good idea!
As the gloomy winter sky got darker, I found myself walking through an eerie graveyard. As I reached the centre of the graveyard, my dog stood still and started barking at a vague, ghostly statue in the distance. Without hesitation, I turned around and sprinted through the forsaken graveyard, fighting to catch my breath.
I finally started to see the brightness of streetlights and hear the sounds of traffic. Safe, finally!

Megan Burke (10)
Garrett Hall Primary School, Tyldesley

A SCARY DREAM

During a happy summer holiday, my neighbour,
Candy, left. Candy was my friend, but she moved
house. I would miss her.
Two months later, I have a new neighbour. He
looks so cool and weird. I think he has many
secrets. When I am going home I always can see
he is crying.
One day, he says, "I can tell you all about me, but
you can't tell anyone." How strange is that? I can
feel it; he is very lonely and sad. And he changes
into a ghost...
It is all a dream, but what a scary dream...

Charlotte Chan (11)
Garrett Hall Primary School, Tyldesley

A NIGHTMARE

"Help! Someone help!" Fireheart cried, scraping against the stone. He was dangling on a ledge above an endless, dark pit. Fireheart saw blood splatter in front of him and all of a sudden, he fell down... Fireheart awoke in the warriors' den.
"Could you keep it down?" meowed Sandstorm. "Some of us are trying to sleep." Sandstorm rested her head on her paws.
Fireheart heard a blood-curdling yowl and rushed out into the clearing, but what he saw made him feel sick. In front of him, he saw Bluestar (Thunderclan's leader) and Spottedleaf (Thunderclan's medicine cat), bloody and dead.
"Noo!"...

Veronica Henning (10)
Grangefield Primary School, Bishops Cleeve

ALICE AND THE ARROW

Alice was standing there with Richard, holding a dazzling ring in his hands. She couldn't believe this snobby man wanted to marry her! Then, Alice saw the most peculiar sight; there, sitting, was a rabbit in a waistcoat (a very stylish waistcoat), and holding a pocket watch! Alice inadvertently ran off to follow it, astonished by this creature. The rabbit stopped by a hole. *Swoosh!* An arrow shot from behind her, heading towards the rabbit! Spinning around, Alice saw Richard holding a bow in his hand. Turning back, the rabbit was gone. Just a trail of scarlet red blood...

Victoria Henning (10)
Grangefield Primary School, Bishops Cleeve

A SNOWMAN'S WISH

Once, there was a snowman who lived in the North Pole.
One cold, starry night, a star shone brightly in the cold winter sky. A snow angel appeared and she said, "I will grant you a wish!"
The snowman said, "I wish to come alive and meet Santa."
The next morning, when he woke, he thought he had had a dream, until a little robin appeared, holding a scarf. He said, "You will need to stay warm on your trip to see Santa. Follow me." He followed the robin through the snow to Santa's village to fulfil his Christmas wish.

Isla Foley (9)
Grangefield Primary School, Bishops Cleeve

NO WAY OUT!

Just another Monday skating home from work when a car screeched around a corner and, losing focus, he fell off his skateboard. Preparing to land on concrete, he landed on a damp carpet, falling unconscious.
An hour later, he awoke to buzzing lights. Realising he was trapped, he began to adventure.
About four hours later, he was so tired he flopped on the floor and slept.
After gaining consciousness, he expected to wake up in his apartment but was greeted with the same buzzing and realised there was no escape from the wet, moist, yellow halls of this disgusting place...

Jake Gray (10)
Great Wakering Primary Academy, Great Wakering

THE THREE PIGS - A TWIST!

One night, in a forest, three pigs were building houses out of straw, sticks and bricks. When the pigs were done, the sheep said, "I'll huff and I'll puff and I'll blow your house down!" The pig got scared but the house didn't blow down so he tried the stick house. "I'll huff and I'll puff and I'll blow your house down!" The house tipped... but stayed up! Maybe he could try the brick house! He blew as hard as he could and... the house was gone! The pigs were very upset pigs...

James Hewitt (10)

Great Wakering Primary Academy, Great Wakering

THE SUPERHEROES AROSE AND WENT DOWN

There were four superheroes called Milly, Molly, George and Billy. At home, they were getting ready for school and planning how to defeat the villains. They saw the news. A new villain had come to Earth. His name was Dr Vigorous. The superheroes got into action and tried to defeat the villain, but they got hit.
When they were at the hospital, Milly was missing! Molly was so worried, so after their treatment, they built a spaceship and flew off.
Milly was there waiting on Pluto. The superheroes looked confused. Milly knocked the superheroes out and finished off the superheroes.

Tofunmi Alubankudi (10)
Heritage Park Primary School, Park Farm

THE CHEESY JOURNEY

Percy Pig, Pickle Panda and Derek Dog were best friends. A mysterious beam of light appeared. The curious trio of creatures they were, they went to investigate. They approached the blinding light and heard a piercing noise. Suddenly, they started to float towards the clouds. They saw a humongous spaceship.
Once through the clouds, they were teleported to an intergalactic planet. Derek Dog became peckish and decided he needed a snack, not knowing the planet was made of cheese. Derek almost ate the entire planet. He became so inflated, Percy and Pickle got on his back to ride home.

Anya Crane (10)
Heritage Park Primary School, Park Farm

THE THREE LITTLE PIGS

The three little pigs built houses. They were made out of straw, sticks and bricks.
One day, a big bad wolf came and blew down all the houses. The straw one, the stick one and the brick one. The big bad wolf ate all three little pigs. He ate the first one, the second one and even the third one. The big bad wolf had won. He lived happily ever after.

Ellaa Ghirani (8)
Heritage Park Primary School, Park Farm

DREAMER

Ruff! Ruff!

"Argh! There's a dog chasing me!"

Maria was running so fast you could hear her heart beating like a drum. Her friend, Emma, joined her as they tried to get away from the dog as soon as possible. As the fearsome dog came closer to her she started to panic. Max, her neighbour came running... Black! Silence!

They soon found themselves trapped in a pitch-black hole. They all yelled, "Help!" Nobody responded or came. Maria fell unconscious. *Bam!*

Maria sat up in her bed. She sighed with relief that she had just been dreaming.

Riya Chana (9)

Hewens Primary School, Hayes

A COOL MINECRAFT DREAM

One day NatiOMG went on a mining adventure. Surprisingly, her whole world was diamonds. She started mining and was extremely happy until she noticed that it wasn't diamonds but dirt. Luckily, she had a brilliant idea to use commands and typed in: 'Give NatiOMG 1000,000 diamonds'. Sadly, it didn't work. Suddenly, she stopped and realised that something wasn't right. She started glitching like in a video game. NatiOMG started to freak out as it was turning dark and had nothing but dirt. She heard a voice. She opened her eyes. It was all just a wonderful but weird dream.

Natalia Dolecka (9)
Hewens Primary School, Hayes

THE LIAR

There once was a good girl named Suna. She was new to a boarding school. She met a boy named Jacob. He became her friend.
One night they were playing. Jacob kept winning. All of a sudden, the gushing wind broke her window. They were both so scared. Suna ran to hide. She looked for Jacob but he was nowhere to be seen. A few seconds later, he appeared with red bloody eyes. He slowly walked to her. She was terrified...
She was nowhere to be seen. What do you think happened to her? Is she safe, unsafe or gone?

Anayah Khan (9)
Hewens Primary School, Hayes

THE MISSING CHILD

A little girl and her family moved to a new town.
They loved it! But there were a lot of creeps about
at night, so they tried to not go out so much.
Milly went out all the time by herself. She also
sneaked out as well. Tonight, she was going to
meet up with her online friend, Ruby. Ruby was an
evil witch, Milly didn't know that tho... Tonight,
they were going out for the first time with each
other. Milly got kidnapped by Ruby. She tried to
poison her.
Luckily, she got home safely because of her dad.

Ella Wanless (10)
Homerswood Primary School, Kirklands

FANCY A LETTER?

"P-please, d-does anyone have any money?" shivered Lola because it was cold.
"Another day with nothing, Daniel," said Lola sadly.
Yawn! "Another morning, another day," Lola muttered.
"What! There is 100,000 pounds just here!" exclaimed Lola. "We can get a house," she exclaimed happily.
"I didn't know doing paperwork was so hard," Lola said. "I know it's only been a day but let's go check the mailbox," said Lola. "Okay it seems like someone's watching me," said Lols frightened. "I hope I don't get another letter..."
Would this happen again?

Jessica Gladman (10)
Hurst Primary School, Bexley

CINDERELLA AND THE TRAGIC ENDING

A girl called Cinderella heard about a ball. The prince was going to be there so she asked if she could go but her father said, "No you need to stay home and scrub the floors!"
So on that day, her sisters got to go, but her sisters started bragging so Cinderella ran upstairs and cried. Then a fairy with a carriage, dress and glass slippers appeared so she got ready and left. But when she got to the ball, the magic wore off so then everyone laughed at her, and so did the prince. She then ran back home.

Grace Henderson (10)
Hurst Primary School, Bexley

THREE LITTLE PIGS AND A WOLF

There were three pigs. They all went to the city. In the city, the first pig said, "Can I buy some straw please?"
"Yes," said the man.
He went to build a house. There were only two pigs left and they went to buy wood to build their home and number three went to a brick shop and then they all went home.
A big wolf came and blew the straw house down and went to the wood house and blew that down then they went to the brick house. The wolf couldn't blow that down so they played.

Kitty Brown (9)
Hurst Primary School, Bexley

THE MISSING DAD

One day, a girl called Bella lived with her mum because her dad left her when she was young. She went to school every day and her favourite teacher was called Mr Pen. Bella was really smart and she was trying to find her dad. One time she found a picture of him in her mum's drawer. She thought the face was familiar. She would recognise those dimples anywhere. Maybe it was Mr Pen. No, he had brown hair! My dad had blond hair. No, it can't be him!
Could my dad be Mr Pen, my teacher?

Ruby Rose (10)
Hurst Primary School, Bexley

THE THREE LITTLE PIGS

The three little pigs had to leave their mum's house. So the three little pigs walked and walked together. The first pig saw straw and got building his house. The second pig saw sticks and wood and got to work. The third pig saw bricks and also got to work. One day a wolf came and saw the pigs. He was very hungry so he huffed and puffed and blew. The straw house was gone and the stick house. So the pigs ran to the next. The brick house didn't get destroyed so the wolf ate their mum!

Louis Downey (9)
Hurst Primary School, Bexley

THE SWAMPS OF MALEFICENT AND AURORA

Everything you have heard is a lie! In a swamp far away lived a girl called Aurora but she was Gothic. There also lived a nice, kind girl called Maleficent. She lived in a wonderful, brightly-coloured swamp. She was a fairy like a pixie. One day Maleficent found a girl she had never seen before, her name was Aurora. Aurora was a wicked girl. She would rip her teddy bears in half and she liked being pricked by things. She also loved black clothing...

Millie Harris (9)
Hurst Primary School, Bexley

LORD BIN THE FOURTH BEST BIRTHDAY

Once on an alien planet, Lord Bin the Fourth (who is Bin for short), wanted pickled pickles for lunch, so Bin went to the Pickled Picks Shop (which sells pickled stuff) but when he got there it was closed. "Pickled potatoes!" he yelled. So Bin went back to his castle because if the shop is closed, how is he going to get his pickled pickles?

As he opened the door to his castle, "Surprise party!" yelled his friends. "We got you a pickled pickles cake as we know you love pickled pickles. Happy birthday to you Lord Bin the Fourth."

Iris Van Alphen (10)

Lancaster Steiner School, Lancaster

HOUSE

"Bye, Mum!" I shouted whilst bursting out the door straight to the shed to carry on making my spaceship. I had a box to make it.
While I was making it I heard a strange noise.
Aliens! "Miranda, come here," I shouted. My dog, Miranda, burst out the door, jumping all over me.
"Come, let's investigate where the sound is coming from."
I ran out the gate, Miranda following on. I knocked on my neighbour's door to see something despicable. The house was full of random gadgets and at the door was an alien...

Lilly Crawshaw (10)

Lower Kersal Community Primary School, Salford

THE DEMON IN THE CASTLE

One cold day, John invited his friends to his house. After welcoming, they watched TV. The news showed a castle that was forbidden. John thought it was a myth. After his friends left, John went to bed.

The next day, John went to the park with his friend. As they were going home, John found a map to the castle. He told his friends. They went with him but they didn't know that Jack was the demon.

After entering the castle, Jack disappeared. The friends were scared. The demon came. They shouted... Jack showed himself. Jack killed them...

Daniel Olatunji (9)

Lower Kersal Community Primary School, Salford

BEACH DISASTER

Hi, I'm Sandra and this is my story. One lovely day I decided to go to the beach, what a mistake. I was just relaxing on the golden sand when I started to hear a rumbling sound. I glanced up and saw a bolt of lightning strike! "Strange but oh well." Wait, it was getting colder. "Brr!"
I got up with my towel and thought *not the day for me, I suppose. What a disaster.* Just then I got struck by lightning and my vision went black.
The next day I heard that it was all just a dream...

Lola Clarke (10)
Lower Kersal Community Primary School, Salford

LITTLE RED RIDING HOOD

One day Red Riding Hood told her dad she was off to see Grandma for a couple of days. But Dad couldn't walk her through the forest and she was petrified of the forest. So when she left she dashed through the forest and got to Grandma's spooky house quicker than usual.
When she got to Grandma's she opened the door. Her grandma wasn't there, she thought. After 30 minutes, she was getting bored. So she opened the closet door and saw Grandma with a tarnished axe in her hand...

Alex Statham (11)
Lower Kersal Community Primary School, Salford

URSULA'S GREAT RETURN

"No! She's Ursula!"
The sun was setting and the curse began to lift.
Ursula kissed the prince, making him fall in love with her.
Meanwhile, on the wood deck, Ariel was transformed into her mermaid form. To make sure Ariel couldn't get in the way Ursula took her voice and banished her to the deepest, darkest depths of the ocean, never to be seen again...

Toby Keogh (10)
Lower Kersal Community Primary School, Salford

NIGHTMARE

It was a dark, gloomy night. The streets were lonely and quiet, I was surrounded by darkness. I was feeling scared. Suddenly, I heard a demonic voice coming towards me.

It was a manly voice saying "You are next."

Each second, the voice kept on getting louder. It made me feel frightened. *Bang!* I heard a loud noise. I looked around and saw a man staring at me. His eyes were bleeding red and his mouth was covered in blood. It was too late. *Buzz buzz!* My alarm went off. I woke up in sweat. It was all a nightmare...

Muskaan Faisal (9)
Margaret McMillan Primary School, Heaton

THE GRINCH

When the Grinch woke up, he looked out of the window. It was Christmas. He hated Christmas with his dog Max. All the lights were glowing. He hated it but he took a closer look and saw Santa Claus. He ran downstairs with a master plan. He made big, springy shoes.
Max said, "Is that the real Santa?"
The Grinch said, "Yes! Tomorrow, we will steal all the presents."
He was stealing all the presents, but Santa saw him. He chased him in his sleigh. He took him to a humongous Christmas tree. The Grinch got caught and said sorry.

Ryan McMillan (9)
Mauricewood Primary School, Greenlaw Mains

ANGEL AND STITCH

Angel and Stitch were out surfboarding and there were huge waves in the sea. A huge wave came and hit them and they lost their surfboards in the sea. They got split up. One of them went one way and the other went the other way. They were lost in the sea. Suddenly, Angel got stung by a jellyfish. It started to get dark and there were stars in the sky. Both of them were getting tired. They looked around them one more time. Both of them saw land. They swam to the land. They were safe...

Gracie-Beau Rorison (9)

Mauricewood Primary School, Greenlaw Mains

THE GETAWAY

Alarms rang. Terry waited in the car for his gang to appear. They had stolen the famous Pimpernel diamond from the Russians. Unfortunately, Terry chose a Trabant, and it broke down.
The gang had no choice but to run. The police caught everyone and sent them to the Gulag. Everyone except for Terry. Terry now charters fishing boats in Hawaii.
One day a strangely familiar passenger appears. Caiser, one of his old gang members. Terry panics and tries to escape. But it is too late. Interpol are waiting on the dock. Caiser exchanged his life for Terry and the diamond.

Ciara Lauren Harrison (11)
Middleton Park School, Bridge Of Don

LITTLE RED RIDING HOOD GONE WRONG

One day, Little Red Riding Hood was walking through the woods, trembling with fear, when she came across a lumberjack who told her about a giant wolf who was after her and hiding in her grandmother's tiny old cottage. She thanked the lumberjack and carried on walking. When she arrived at the door, she was terrified. She found a shiny axe, picked it up for safety, swung the door open and immediately threw the axe, not just missing the wolf but hitting and decapitating her grandmother. Then Little Red sat down and had a cup of tea with the wolf.

Mollie Redford (10)
Middleton Park School, Bridge Of Don

ON THE ROOMY BROOMY

One chilly autumn morning, Winnie the witch with her clumsy cat was cruising along in the foggy sky on her battered broomstick. Her hair was flapping lazily in the light breeze as she looked around and said to her cat, "For the 127th time, don't lean over the edge, you clumsy creature."
And what did she see when she turned around? Nothing! The cat had plummeted into the earth below and Winnie, not having x-ray vision, could not see her through the dense cloud of fog.

Mustafa Khan (9)
Oasis Academy Hobmoor, Yardley

THE DAY OF LONDON

Felling excited as the sun zoomed inside of my eyes, I arrived at my destination I was so excited to go on all the rides but there was one thing I had to wait for: my friends. While I was waiting I saw lots of cars and trust me it was very busy. All of a sudden my friends gave me a fright. Then a few minutes later we went on all the rides except the Londen Eye. We were waiting and I couldn't believe it, people were pushing and pushing. Then finally we went on the Londen Eye.

Rahana (8)

Oasis Academy Hobmoor, Yardley

THE WOLF AND TWO PIGS

One time there lived a wolf called Will and two pigs called Bob and Bill. Bob and Bill had always wanted to trick Will. One day they decided to prank him. They shouted, "Will, come here."
The wolf ran over.
"Go inside this house. It definitely doesn't have slime in there," said Bill.
"Okay, but you go behind me," said Will.
Bill stood behind him. Will ran back past Bill and Bill slipped and fell in the slime.
"Haha, now you see I'm smarter!"
They never messed with him again and Will lived happily ever after.

Spencer Smith (8)
Ringstead CE Primary School, Ringstead

100 NINJAS

There are 100 Ninjas trying to beat Shrek.
Who do you think is going to win?
Shrek or 100 Ninjas?
On a wild, windy night, 100 Ninjas sneaked up on Shrek and the battle began!
Ninjas kicked and punched with 40 ninjas left, Shrek got defeated.
They went back to Ninja Village. The training had begun. They got more powerful. The Ninjas started to hear local villagers whispering how Shrek had been spotted but not on his own.
200 Ninjas sprinted off and found Shrek at the top of the hill with an ally!
Who do you think will win?

Cayden Murphy (9)
Saints & Scholars Integrated Primary School, Armagh

EMMA GOES TO THE ZOO

There once was a girl called Emma, and her class was going on a trip to the zoo. When they got there, it was lunchtime, and a monkey stole her banana. Everyone thought it was very funny. Next stop was the lion cage, but it escaped and they didn't know it was a haunted zoo, but it didn't stop them. They found the lion. One of the students touched it and it bit off her hand. She was rushed to the hospital and the zookeeper said, "We are very sorry!" That has happened and again, we are very sorry.

Aimèe White (9)

Saints & Scholars Integrated Primary School, Armagh

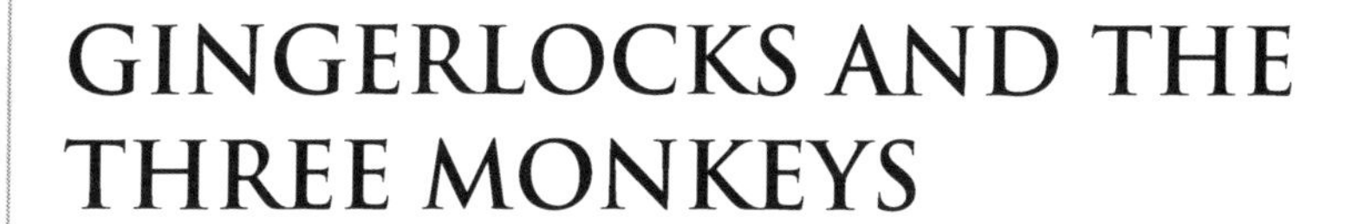

GINGERLOCKS AND THE THREE MONKEYS

Once, there was a little girl named Gingerlocks who used to steal food. She did this a lot! In the woods lived three sneaky monkeys who had a plan to stop Gingerlocks for good! The three monkeys climbed up to the top of the tallest tree armed with bowls of hot, thick, sticky porridge. Silently they waited until they saw Gingerlocks approaching their house. Then the monkeys put their plan into action. They threw the hot sticky porridge at Gingerlocks and watched as it set hard as stone, freezing Gingerlocks in that spot forever! The monkeys' food was safe!

Karter Smith (8)
St Helens PACE PRU, Parr

THE MAGICIAN

One boring old school day, a class went on a school trip to a magic festival. They were all super excited and were jumping up and down in their bus seats, not keeping still.
It was all going well until there was long traffic and the bus ran out of fuel. At that time, cars were all about and the bus driver had no internet. The children were panicking as they tried to call for help, but nobody answered.
They were stranded there until it was night-time. Nobody was awake until somebody was heard crying in the gloomy forest...

Posi Olaoye (10)
St John Rigby Catholic Primary School, Bedford

GOLDILOCKS AND HER SCARIEST DAY

Goldilocks was walking in the forest and she saw a house. Then she went into the house. She saw three bowls of porridge but she didn't eat them because she could see they were hot, cold, and poisonous!
She went upstairs, then she saw the bears. She saw Baby Bear going downstairs, so she hid under a table. Then the dad came, he was enormous. She sneaked downstairs. Then she saw the mum bear. She ran outside and they chased her. Then Goldilocks escaped.

Seyar Kamal (10)
St Paul's CE Primary School, Brentford

THE THREE LITTLE PANDAS AND THE NAUGHTY KANGAROO

In the brick house in the Amazon Rainforest, three little pandas lived. Surprisingly, they had four bedrooms, three bathrooms and a kitchen. One day they went out for a walk. Suddenly, they saw a raccoon. They were confused. Surprisingly, it yelled something. "There is a bad kangaroo that has trapped a poor guinea pig."
When they heard this they suddenly went to the house and saved the guinea pig. They whacked the kangaroo and all of his teeth fell out. The pandas had a nice tea party with the guinea pig and the kangaroo went back to Australia.

Paddy Stapleton (9)
St Peter's CE Primary School, South Weald

THE GINGERBREAD MAN

One day a woman was baking a gingerbread man and went to get some sparkling icing but it was actually a potion. Suddenly he came alive, jumped out of the window and ran away thinking he was safe. Then he noticed a cat, dog and rat were looking at him hungrily. He started to run but they followed him. He then saw a farmer, a fisherman and a shepherd running after him. A fox slowly approached and asked him to hop on his back so he did. They went to a secret base and became the best of friends.

Maya Challice (9)

St Peter's CE Primary School, South Weald

CLEETUS AND THE EVIL FRIEND

As Cleetus walked through the dark cave with his friend, he felt a bad feeling... Then, all of a sudden, his friend touched a glowing rock. He started to grow, his eyes turned glowing red... Meanwhile, Cleetus was holding his pet rock. He pressed his 'merge' button... Then, all of a sudden, Cleetus turned into a fighter! The two battled a good fight then Cleetus turned to human by accident... but he had a plan... He grabbed a sword and his evil friend was so scared he turned away and ran! Cleetus had saved the day!

Olly Pomfrey (9)
Stafford Junior School, Eastbourne

THE MYSTERIOUS MAN

There was a man who was mysterious. He was turning into dust because he didn't believe in himself. When he was young, he was bullied. When he was 22, he saw someone he knew. "I am confused," he said. His friend had moved to the USA when he was young. The person knocked on his door. He said he had moved to the USA to help give support. On the 29th of January, he went to university and became a Doctor. He now knows that you need to believe in yourself.

Ben Walton (11)

Strathpeffer Primary School, Strathpeffer

THE SINISTER RED RIDING HOOD TWIST

Between the sea and the sky, Lucy always went to see her grandpa after school, every day. Grandpa did not know that Lucy was mean and cruel.
One day after school, Lucy went to her grandpa's house and said, "Hello, Grandpa, I have bought you some bread to eat."
Grandpa replied, "Thank you!"
She immediately grabbed her grandpa's hand and tried to kill him. Luckily a young man heard a loud noise and, as fast as a flash, the young man appeared in front of Lucy and trapped her in the house. He called the police. They took Lucy away.

Ayea Othman (10)
The Baird Primary Academy, Hastings

THE CREEPY NEIGHBOUR

In a little neighbourhood, 27 Little Bridge Road, there was a little girl who was 14 years old and named Lilly. She was looking out of her window then, out of the corner of her eye, she saw a moving truck pull into her old neighbour's driveway. Just then Lilly remembered that she was getting a new neighbour. Later that evening, Lilly heard something from her window. It was her new neighbour, she was wearing a tight-fitted jacket. Lilly followed the neighbour. She put on her fluffy coat and left her house. The neighbour was leading her to a door...

Mia Isted (11)

The Baird Primary Academy, Hastings

THE MUFFIN MAN

Occasionally you will hear the muffin man song.
Here is the true story...
It was 1882, London, Little Timmy was very poor.
He searched the roads for food. He asked for money, he rarely got much. It had been months since he got money or food but he saw a man with many muffins. Timmy gave him a nickname: The Muffin Man. He saw him every day luring children in. He'd always come back in something red. One day Timmy said, "Hello, who are you really?" He grabbed Timmy's arm, killed Timmy and made him into a muffin!

Stanley Page (10)
The Baird Primary Academy, Hastings

FOX AND SEAGULL BATTLE

At first, the fox was just looking for food but the seagull that pecked at it interfered. The Fox began to resist but the seagull was a bird. The fox decided to jump on it and kill it but the Seagull understood the intentions of the fox and he called his friends and the Fox ran away. Then that same Fox told the captain fox about what had happened and, it turned out, that this fox was the wife of the captain fox! The captain fox was very angry and decided to attack the city of seagulls! They destroyed them.

Muhammad Khashiev (11)
The Baird Primary Academy, Hastings

THE CAT AND THE KITTEN

Once upon a time, there was a cat and kitten who went to school together. One morning the teacher discovered that the test answers had been stolen. The teacher checked everyone's bag to see who the culprit was. She checked the sneaky snake's bag first... there was nothing. Then she checked the cunning croc, angry cat, cheeky gorilla... but none of them had the test answers. Finally, she checked the little kitten's bag and discovered the test papers. The little kitten was sent home and never came back again. All the other animals lived happily ever after.

Phoebe Mok (8)
The Study School, New Malden

THE SCHOOL BUS

The ride begins. I am on the old, yellow school bus with my friends. It is a normal, boring day. I look out of the window and find that the bus is soaring through the blue sky. Everyone is screaming and having a great time. Eventually we encounter a monster charging through the air towards us with short hair and massive talons.
I hear a voice calling, "Please vacate the ride!"
Everyone disappears but me. I am on my own. I can no longer see the amusement park. The monster approaches...

Seth Mckenna (10)
The Study School, New Malden

SNUGGLES

A long time ago on a planet on the edge of the galaxy lived a boy called Snuggles. One day Snuggles found a fossil. At first he thought it was just a rock. But it was a dinosaur called a pterosaur, a type of bird. "Meep!" went the pterosaur. "Meep, meep, meep, meep." Snuggles hopped on and *whoosh!* Snuggles found himself in China, Japan and Mexico. A lot of people were jealous. So they planned an attack. The tanks came first...

Harry Dawson (9)
The Study School, New Malden

THE PTERODACTYL'S TWIST

One early morning, there was a pterodactyl sleeping in his dark, deep cave. He was on top of a mountain. Suddenly a potion fell off the mountain. The pterodactyl decided to chase it. So he went down the mountain. He picked it up and drank it. He started to feel bad and then he turned really fast. Later that day, the pterodactyl got stuck in a hole. He saw a handprint and touched it. Another animal came. He had a fight against him and he won. He saved so many children and people he was so proud of himself.

Ollie Clarke (10)
Winsford High Street CP School, Winsford

THE MYSTERY DIARY

Dear Diary,
Henry Peboa found my diary. He started writing. I responded. Mr Peboa got sucked in. He started telling me his own story...
"I fell down into the Chamber of Snakes. I met the Ksilasab. Along with falling, I found the cloak of mystery, Gilly Gamsé gem and Badgers crown... but I couldn't find the ring. I found it on Violet. I started to fight Violet's creature. The battle had now commenced..."
Henry won the fight... for the first time. He fought me and now I'm now in my diary talking to myself one more time!
Violet Lilac.

Elliesha Khan (10)
Wyndham Spencer Academy, Alvaston

SANTA SWAP!

A weird coincidence happened on Christmas Eve. Santa's workshop got tricked by a cheeky and mischievous elf. Santa fell over a trip wire that was placed by the fireplace. He could no longer deliver presents. Surprisingly someone not very Christmassy came to save Christmas. The guy who had stolen Christmas was back to save it... the Grinch! Out of all the people, the Christmas hater was gonna save Christmas. If he could steal it, he could definitely save it! He started the sleigh and took off. Could the Grinch do this? Could it work out? We will never know...

Darcey Rule (9)
Wyndham Spencer Academy, Alvaston

MAGIC AND ENCHANTMENT

The shimmering ball caught Alice's eye, she picked it up and ran home. While running home she fell and broke it. She didn't want anyone to find out. She tried to clean the goo that oozed out of the broken glass ball. When she was cleaning up her mess, Alice noticed something peculiar... The goo shone every time she touched it. She thought it was cool and took it home. Little did she know, it would turn her into something odd... She at last reached home and looked in her mirror. She was... a superhero? She kept her secret forever.

Kaede Lightoller (9)
Wyndham Spencer Academy, Alvaston

Young Writers Information

We hope you have enjoyed reading this book – and that you will continue to in the coming years.

If you're the parent or family member of an enthusiastic poet or story writer, do visit our website **www.youngwriters.co.uk/subscribe** and sign up to receive news, competitions, writing challenges and tips, activities and much, much more! There's lots to keep budding writers motivated!

If you would like to order further copies of this book, or any of our other titles, then please give us a call or order via your online account.

Young Writers
Remus House
Coltsfoot Drive
Peterborough
PE2 9BF
(01733) 890066
info@youngwriters.co.uk

Join in the conversation!
Tips, news, giveaways and much more!

YoungWritersUK YoungWritersCW youngwriterscw

Scan me to watch the A Twist In The Tale video!